Billie B. Brown

Birthday Girl!!

PARTY

www.BillieBBrownBooks.com

Billie B. Brown Books

The Bad Butterfly
The Soccer Star
The Midnight Feast
The Second-best Friend
The Extra-special Helper
The Beautiful Haircut
The Big Sister
The Spotty Vacation
The Birthday Mix-up
The Secret Message
The Little Lie
The Best Project

First American Edition 2013
Kane Miller, A Division of EDC Publishing

Text Copyright © 2011 Sally Rippin
Illustrations Copyright © 2011 Aki Fukuoka
Logo and design copyright © 2011 Hardie Grant Egmont

First published in Australia in 2011 by Hardie Grant Egmont

For information contact:
Kane Miller, A Division of EDC Publishing
P.O. Box 470663
Tulsa, OK 74147-0663
www.kanemiller.com
www.edcpub.com
www.usbornebooksandmore.com

Library of Congress Control Number: 2012956109
Printed and bound in the United States of America
2 3 4 5 6 7 8 9 10
ISBN: 978-1-61067-182-8

Billie B. Brown

The Birthday Mix-up

By Sally Rippin

Illustrated by Aki Fukuoka

Kane Miller
A DIVISION OF EDC PUBLISHING

Chapter One

Billie B. Brown has ten invitations, two packages of balloons and one box of colored pencils. Do you know what the "B" in Billie B. Brown stands for?

Birthday.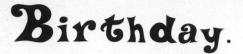

Soon it will be Billie
B. Brown's birthday.
Isn't that exciting?

Billie is allowed to
invite ten friends to her
birthday party. This is
very hard for Billie.
There are twenty-one
people in her class.

Ten invitations

One box of
colored pencils

Two packages
of balloons

PARTY

3

Billie wants to invite everyone, but her mom and dad say no, no and NO. They say ten noisy kids is plenty!

Billie is writing out her invitations. Jack is helping her decide who to invite to her party. Jack is Billie's best friend. He lives next door.

"I know!" Billie says, counting on her fingers. "There are exactly ten girls in our class, not including me. I will just invite the girls."

Jack frowns. "What about me?" he says.

"Oh," says Billie. "Of course."

Billie can't have a party without Jack!

"Well, maybe I won't invite Lola. She can be very annoying," Billie says. "How about nine girls and one boy?"

"Then Lola will be the only girl not invited," says Jack. "She won't like that. You'll hurt her feelings. And then she will be cross."

"You're right," says Billie.

"Maybe you should invite five girls and five boys?" Jack says. "That's fair."

"Good idea," says Billie. But it's still no good. Billie can only think of four boys she would like to invite. The other boys are just too **loud** and silly.

Oh dear. What a headache!

In the end, Billie decides to invite four boys and six girls.

Billie's mom writes everything on a piece of paper for Billie to copy. Her mom has to write quickly because Billie's baby brother, Noah, is hungry.

She writes:

Saturday 4th April 12:30pm

Billie copies out all the invitations in colored pencil.

Here is one of Billie's invitations. Doesn't it look pretty?

PARTY

DEAR Poppy

PLEASE COME TO MY PARTY!

DATE: Saturday 4th Afi April

TIME: 2:30 pm

FROM: Billie

11

Chapter Two

It is only five sleeps
until Billie's party.
She is very **excited**.
Each day at school she
checks that everyone
is coming.

She has to whisper because she doesn't want the kids who aren't invited to feel left out.

"Are you coming to my party this Saturday?" Billie whispers to Poppy in class.

"Yes!" says Poppy.
"You've asked me ten
times already, Billie."

"Are you getting me a
present?" Billie asks.

"Billie, Poppy, no
whispering in class,"
Ms. Walton says.

But Billie is so **excited**
she can hardly keep still.

"My goodness," Ms. Walton says. "Did you eat jumping beans for breakfast, Billie?"

Ms. Walton makes Billie sit in the front row because she won't stop wriggling.

Every afternoon, Billie and Jack plan the games that they will play at Billie's party.

Billie has a special purple notebook where she writes down the list of games. Every day it changes.

Soon the list looks like this:

~~Soccer X~~

Pass-the-parcel //

~~Cubbies~~ Cubbies /

Disco dancing ? B=yes ~~J=no~~

Soccer /

~~Chasey Kiss chasey~~ X Chasey / ~~(boys against girls)~~ X

Catch the flag //   Musical chairs /

Every night, Billie
asks her mom and dad
how many sleeps until
her party.

Every night her dad
says, "One sleep less
than the last time you
asked, Billie."

"Don't worry, Billie,"
says her mom.

"Nobody is going to forget your party!"

But Billie lies in bed and **worries**.

What if they don't like the games? she thinks. *What if they don't like the food? What if the boys won't play with the girls? Or worst of all, what if... nobody comes?*

Chapter Three

Finally, it is Saturday.
Billie rushes into her
mom and dad's bedroom
to see if they are awake.
Billie's mom is sitting up
feeding Noah.

Her dad is fast asleep.
Billie jumps up and down
on the bed to wake him.

Billie's dad rubs his
eyes and yawns. Then he
reaches under the bed and
pulls out their birthday
presents for Billie.

"Happy birthday, Billie!"
her mom and dad say.

Billie opens her presents.

She has lots of lovely things.

She feels very lucky.

"Careful. Don't let
Noah eat the paper!" her
mom laughs.

Billie and Noah and
their mom and dad have
a big birthday cuddle on
the bed.

Suddenly Billie sits up.

"What time is it?" she asks. "Is it nearly time for my party?"

"No, Billie, you have lots of time," her mom says. "Your friends aren't coming until twelve-thirty. Besides, you're going to Jack's for a special birthday breakfast, remember?"

"Twelve-thirty!" says Billie.

"That's ages away. Can I stay and play with Jack after breakfast?"

"OK," says Billie's mom. "Dad and I will get up soon and get ready for the party."

Billie puts on her bathrobe and runs downstairs and out into the backyard.

Then she squeezes
through the hole in the
fence into Jack's backyard.

Jack is sitting at his
kitchen table. Billie knocks
on the back door.

"Come in," says Jack's
mom. "Happy birthday,
Billie! We're making your
favorite breakfast. Banana
pancakes!"

"Yum!" says Billie.

Jack's mom makes
a special plate
of banana
pancakes for
Billie, with
honey and
sprinkles.

Jack gives Billie a present.
It is a Lego set! Just what
she wanted.

Billie and Jack sit in the family room and build a super-duper rocket ship.

Suddenly, Billie looks up. "What time is it?" she asks.

"Quarter past twelve," says Jack.

"Quick!" says Billie. "Everyone will be here soon! I have to get ready!"

Billie and Jack run next door to Billie's house. Billie goes upstairs and puts on her special party dress. Then she runs downstairs to the kitchen.

"Just in time!" says Billie's mom, smiling. "Everything is all ready for your party. Dad is just putting Noah to sleep.

Why don't you two sit on the front step to wait for everyone?"

"Yay!" say Billie and Jack. They run outside.

"What time is it?" says Billie.

Jack looks at his watch. "It's twelve-thirty," he says. "Anyone from now on is officially late!"

Billie giggles. "Don't worry, they'll be here soon. I checked with everyone and they all said they were coming."

Billie and Jack wait.

They wait and they wait and they wait.

But nobody comes.

Chapter Four

"What time is it now, Jack?"
Billie asks in a little voice.

Jack looks worried.
He looks down at his
watch. "It's nearly one
o'clock," he says.

Billie frowns. Her friends can't *all* be late.

Then she gets a funny feeling in her tummy. Her bottom lip begins to quiver and a big tear rolls down her face.

Nobody is coming to her birthday party!

Billie's mom comes out the front door. "My goodness!" she says. "They *are* late!"

Billie bursts into tears. "They're not coming!" she cries. "Nobody is coming to my birthday party! Nobody likes me!"

Billie's mom gives Billie
a cuddle. "Did you give
out all the invitations?"
she asks.

"Yes!" sobs Billie.

"Did you check that everyone could make it?" says her mom.

"Yes!" sobs Billie. "Of course I did! Every day!"

Billie cries and cries. This is the worst birthday ever. Not one of her school friends is coming to her party.

"Are you sure you wrote the right date and time on the invitation?" Billie's mom asks. "Saturday the fourth of April at twelve-thirty?"

"Yes, yes and *yes*!" says Billie crying even louder.

But Jack frowns. He looks like he is remembering something.

Can *you* remember?

Jack runs next door. A few minutes later, he runs back to Billie and her mom. He is waving the invitation in his hand and he has a huge smile on his face.

Do you know why?

Go back to have another
look at the invitation.

That's right! Billie wrote
down the wrong time
on the invitations.
Instead of twelve-thirty,
she wrote two-thirty!

Billie's mom wrote so quickly that Billie couldn't read her writing properly.

Of course her friends are coming!

Billie wipes her eyes and laughs loudly. Jack and Billie's mom laugh too. What a mix-up!

Play cool games and visit Billie at

www.BillieBBrownBooks.com